Thomas Chalmers

The Juvenile Revival

Thomas Chalmers

The Juvenile Revival

ISBN/EAN: 9783337375522

Printed in Europe, USA, Canada, Australia, Japan

Cover: Foto ©Andreas Hilbeck / pixelio.de

More available books at **www.hansebooks.com**

THE JUVENILE REVIVAL;

OR

THE PHILOSOPHY OF THE CHRISTIAN ENDEAVOR MOVEMENT.

BY THOMAS CHALMERS, Ph. D.,

Pastor of the Church of Christ, Brooklyn, N. Y.

Author of "Alexander Campbell in Scotland."

WITH AN INTRODUCTION BY FRANCIS E. CLARK, D. D.

" Like a tree planted by the rivers of water, that bringeth
forth his fruit in his season; his leaf also *shall not wither*."

St. Louis:

CHRISTIAN PUBLISHING COMPANY,

1893.

CONTENTS.

(3)

INTRODUCTION.

So far as I have been able to examine the advance sheets of this volume, I am glad to heartily express my appreciation of its usefulness and unique value. The Society of Christian Endeavor is very often looked at from the practical standpoint, and its actual workings from all sides have been examined, criticised, defended, and for the most part cordially commended, by pastors and Christian people in all parts of the country. The time has now come, as it seems to me, for more careful examination of the philosophical principles which underlie the movement. Any such organization, which in eleven years has made its way around the world, and numbers among its members nearly a million and a half young people, must have some springs of vitality which do not always bubble to the surface. There must be some underlying principles on which such a movement rests. It cannot be accounted

(5)

for by the gush of youthful enthusiasm. Every religious uprising in the history of the world has had such principles, and though they have not always been clearly apprehended at the beginning, and though the practical necessities have largely overshadowed the philosophical principles on which the movement was based, these principles nevertheless exist. So it is with the Society of Christian Endeavor, and it is well that from the standpoint of an active pastor, who knows experimentally what the society is, what its aims, purposes, methods and tendencies are, such a volume should be written. The philosophy then becomes something more than mere theory. *A priori* reasoning is balanced by practical experience, and the experience confirms and is confirmed by the underlying philosophy. Many will doubtless be interested by such a presentation of the case who might distrust the merely practical exhibit of the working of a single society. I believe the volume is calculated to do much good, and I wish it every success in advancing the cause the author has so warmly at heart, and which he has here so wisely espoused and commended.

FRANCIS E. CLARK.

Boston, Mass.,

I.

THE SOIL.

"It was planted in a goodly soil by great waters, that it might bring forth branches, and that it might bear fruit, that it might be a goodly vine."—*Ezekiel.*

"I hail the young life of our day in religion."
                                        —*Dr. McCosh.*

"Ce qui maitrise le plus fortement ces jeunes intelligences, c'est l'instinct de la relation entre less choses et des racines profondes qu'elles ont dans l'invisible; c'est le sentiment de la solidarite entre les hommes, le besoin de s'associer a cette universelle vibration humaine qui est l'electricite latente du monde moral."—*Vogue's Regards.*

I.

THE SOIL.

A SPIRITUAL plant that has grown in but little more than a decade from a single sprout until its young but giant branches bear the bursting buds of more than a million souls, must have been fortunate, not alone in its planting and culture, but in the good ground from which it sprang. Its fresh and luxuriant vegetation gives evidence as much of the fertility of the soil, as its own structure gives of its species. The soil into which the seed of Christian Endeavor was cast must have been of rich quality. That soil is youthful religious enthusiasm. It is the first and most important objective condition in the marvelous spread of the Christian Endeavor idea. But this susceptibility to religious impression among the young has always existed. From the day

(9)

that Cain and Abel, the first young men, sacrificed to Jehovah of the first fruits of their industry and devotion, no element in human nature has been more evident than juvenile religious enthusiasm—the soil of Christian Endeavor. But the idea or the seed which was planted in this soil has been but recently generated. It sprang up when the conditions and elements united to produce the germination. The time had come when this young enthusiasm should be turned into a newer and purer channel to enrich and irrigate more promising fields in the broad area of the life of the young. Juvenile enthusiasm may then either be compared to the soil, which has existed from the foundation of the world, or the waters which fertilize; the Christian Endeavor idea, either to the seed which grows from the soil, or the channel which gives direction to the stream. The philosophy of the Christian Endeavor phenomenon cannot be comprehended fully without a preliminary study of the characteristics and possibilities of the young mind, as actually shown in a glance over the history of past movements. The revolutions and convulsions of history, the combined results of which have given us our present structure of society, have been, almost without exception, inspired by the zeal and carried onward by the activity of our young men. In the military, political, literary, scientific and religious departments of life, it is the burning, restless spirit of youth which has torn down national walls, amalgamated races, crossed the Alps, reconstructed theology, revolutionized society, literature and science, and then in its unsatisfied and insatiable fire it has wept over the ruins of conquered worlds for other worlds of activity. From Alexander the Great, who led the Macedonian army at the age of seventeen, to Napoleon Bonaparte, who was the greatest general in Europe at the age of twenty-six, the chief warriors of the world were young men; from the boyish Augustus Cæsar, whose wise constructive statesmanship made his reign the memorable Golden Era of Rome, to the younger Pitt, who was Europe's shrewdest statesman when but twenty-five years old, youth has made its activity no less felt in politics than in war. Calvin laid the basis for the theologic thought of more than half the Protestant world when at the age of twenty-five he wrote his Institutes; and it may not be irreverent to remember that the Man of Nazareth was but little more than a youth when he said "It is finished" to a life that has changed the face of humanity and given us a new heaven and a new earth. In our own day the greatest religious movements have begun and grown into power among the young. The Evangelical movement of the eighteenth century, and the Tractarian movement of our own century, had each its origin in the religious fervor of Oxford students. Martin Luther was but thirty-four years old when the signal for the beginning of the Protestant revulsion was sounded by the hammer that nailed the ninety-five theses on the door of the Castle-church in Wittenberg. John Huss was under forty and Savonarola under forty-six when they

died as martyrs to their religious principles after lives full of labors.

We often hear it said that young people
are by nature not religious. Nothing can
be farther from the truth. What is that
pure, disinterested, fervent honesty, the
only normal condition of youth; that
chivalric devotion to reason and right;
that faithfulness to truth as seen, which
often breaks over the boundaries of
parental theology, even at the cost of dis-
inheritance, that pleads the interests of
an unpopular cause and disregards the
jeers of unsympathetic multitudes—what
is that but religion? It may grow restless
and fall asleep under an abstruse discus-
sion on the doctrine of the Holy Trinity;
it may smile at the oddities of ritualism;
it may never have read a written sermon,
or made a formal prayer, or carefully
studied a Scripture passage, but this is no
ground for inferring that youth is lacking
in religious sentiment. It is the very
warmth of the religious nature, its de-
mand for a living ideal, that rebels against
the cold and dry elements in church life.

What shall we call that openness of mind
to new revelations of truth; that susceptibility to conviction; that headlong pursuit of what is real, which never mercena-
rily counts the cost, but goes forward as
if moved by the spirit—what is that but
religion? These are the characteristics of
religion, and they are the characteristics
of youth. Youth has always been religious, but the juvenile religious element
has seldom been recognized or understood, and there has therefore been but
little provision for its cultivation, and its
surplus force and vitality have been
wasted for want of proper channels in
which to exert themselves, and even when
channels have been provided, they have
often been so narrow and shallow that
they could not bear the cargoes of a rich
and full life. Youth must have legitimate
service in which to expend its force, or it
will expend itself in its own dissipation or
in outside destruction. It is like the oxygen which, if received into the lungs, re-
pairs, warms and vitalizes the system; but
if it is shut out, the body dies, and the

same oxygen employs itself in its disintegration.

Lectures to young men, in which the
best and most profusive advice has been
given of what not to do and what to
avoid, from the days of Solomon to the
last volumes issued from the press, have
been well nigh fruitless. We cannot won-
der, when the young men of every age
have been overwhelmed with moraliza-
tions—"Don't do this!" "Don't go
there!" "Don't associate with such!"—
that they have answered in despair, "In
the name of God, what shall we do, where
shall we go, and with whom shall we associate?" When Shakespeare's Henry IV.
is represented by Falstaff as speaking
those kind words of reproof to his son,
"Harry, I do not only marvel where thou
spendest thy time, but also how thou art
accompanied; for though the camomile
the more it is trodden on the faster it
grows, yet youth the more it is wasted the
sooner it wears," he gave good parental
counsel, but the effect of the rebuke
alone would drive the youth into despair

and further profligacy. It was negative truth. But when the activity of war was offered him, this dissipated youth rose

" From the ground like feathered Mercury,"

and, in the hottest of the battle, slew the gallant leader of the Northern rebellion, and when the king begged him to leave the field on account of his wound, it was that same youthful ardor, which a few days before was wasted in drunkenness and revelry, that made the valorous response:

"God forbid a shallow scratch should drive the Prince of Wales from such a field as this, where stained nobility lies trodden on, and rebels' arms triumph in massacres!" Youth longs for noble and legitimate activity, but the flow of its enthusiasm cannot be dammed without disaster. Once upon a time an industrious farmer, through whose small but well planted farm a river ran, took it into his head to increase the area of his arable land; so he dammed the river just outside the boundary fence. On the following morning when he went out, he found that the waters had kept on flowing as before from above, and had flooded and ruined his crops on the lowlands. He removed the dam, and in the course of time built a flour-mill on the banks of the river, and the great waterwheel drove the machinery. His neighbors from miles away brought their grain to his mill, and he grew into great wealth. The water could not be held back, but it would grind his grain, saw his lumber, carry his cargo, and quench his thirst. So it is with youth.

We may as well, then, lay down as a proposition at once that youth cannot be silenced while it is youth. Take its vivacity away, and it is no longer youth. Someone suggests, "Discipline it!" But the trouble is too often that the disciplining process is a destroying, a death-dealing process. *Disciplined* youth is usually as unpromising of fruit as the frost-bitten bud. The broken spirit, the downcast eye, the pallid complexion, the fallen countenance, the slow and regular gait, the nervous lack of self-confidence—these

2

are too often the traces of discipline. It is the bounding step, the sparkling luster of the eye, the quick and willing motion that we want. In the words of Tennyson:

> " 'Tis life whereof our nerves are scant,
> And life not death for which we pant—
> More life and fuller that we want."

"Spare not the rod" is a good word, and should be taken literally. As far as the rod is concerned, it does not need sparing. It may be burned or broken with but little loss to human happiness; but the child should be spared. It is, of course, much easier for parents to handle their children summarily according to "rules laid down," than to trouble themselves with studying sympathetically the nature of the child's soul and surroundings, but is it not the human way? No doubt many will object to a condescension of parent to child as compromising parental dignity, but what is parental dignity? Is it that cold, hard, lofty separation of father from son which has often deprived youth of one of its greatest natural blessings?

While we are talking about the rights of man, woman's rights, the rights of labor and capital, and States' rights, we should not forget that there is also such a doctrine as juvenile rights, and if the young are to be instructed by the old, it should also be remembered that the old may learn much from the young, and this even in religious matters. Is it not "out of the mouths of babes and sucklings" that divine praise finds its most perfect expression?

But a very natural inquiry would be if youth should be let run wild and go down to ruin? There certainly is no need that youth should go wild. That is the opposite error—the falsehood carried about by the emissaries of Satan, who have preached from Adam's time that there is a certain merit in the eating of forbidden fruit, and that free men should live under no restraint. There is no reason why any young man, though perfectly free, should sow tares or wild oats. Those tares are more ruinous to the soil of youth and sap from it more of its fertility and power

than the growth of the grain of legitimate activity. That philosophy is corrupt
and vicious beyond toleration which ac-
cords to young men their youthful years
for dissipation and dissolution, and no
young man who has the courage of manhood or even ordinary prudence or fore-
sight will accept such a proffer. To be
sure, the soil will grow something. If no
good seed is sown, rank weeds and pois-
onous herbs will find their way there, if it
has any fertility; and if it has no fertility
at all, it is as useless to the world as the
Sahara desert. A man who can be a first
class sinner can be something better.
The soil that will grow weeds in healthy
quantities is a promising piece of land.
When our farmers go out West to take
up government land and settle there, they
avoid the dry, desert patches where there
is neither tree, shrub nor weed—nothing
but the clear, white drifting sand,—and
lay claim to the rougher ground, where
weeds in abundance grow. It took " the
Chief of Sinners " to make the Chief of
the Apostles. And yet I know just such

talk as this often exercises a pernicious
influence on the very characters we are
trying to help. The street tough who
hears it will tip his dented hat further on
one side, and, with his hands in his side
pockets, he will walk down street with a
still more self-conscious swagger. He
will drink an extra glass and make a big-
ger stake at the gambling-table. He will
swear a louder oath, and make bolder al-
lusion to the lady that passes by the dry
goods box on which he sits. He will
take it that there is merit in depravity.
He will not compare himself to a crude,
uncultivated patch of land overrun with
malodorous fireweeds, troublesome this-
tles and exasperating briers. Yet, wild
as it is, the ground has promise, but if it
remains always in its native uncultivated
state, it matters little whether it has or
has not promise. So with the sinner, his
very sinfulness, which gives promise of
something better and worthier after his
reformation, makes him, as a sinner, con-
temptible and disgusting.

Man will not be idle. He will serve

either God or Mammon. Nor have we discharged our whole duty when we say: "Choose ye this day whom ye will serve," because church life is oftentimes such that the young man, with his limited religious experience, can see no other service but that of Mammon. There must be a choice before the young man can choose. Mammon has all his wares on exhibition. The gilded saloon, with its odorous and tempting liquors, cards, dice and billiard-tables meets him at every corner. The dazzling theatre, with its throng of frivolous and careless attendants, its insinuatingly immoral plays and "varieties," and sensational costumes calls out loudly through its advertisements in flaming pictures on wagons, buildings, fences, and bulletin boards for the young man's bid. The great majority of the depraved have not chosen sin from preference. They have chosen it from necessity, because church life was either practically out of their reach, or so crystallized and cold that it possessed no charms for them. The preaching has been abstract, and the prayer and social meetings have been insipid and uninteresting, and instead of being greeted by young people of their own age when they appear within the church, they have been recognized and addressed only by the elders or the old ladies. They have been naturally shy and backward, just as they were the first evening they spent in the loud and jolly saloon company, but the latter companionship soon put them at their ease. In a recent article in the *Forum* on the "Impending Paganism in New England," the following picture of the church life in a little New England town is given: "The strongest churches are the Universalist, with its membership of thirteen women, and one man, and the Congregational, with its membership of twenty-seven women and four men. There is hardly a representative man in these four churches, though the Masonic lodge gathers from this and neighboring towns its hundred members." The fault is not in the soil but in its cultivation.

I repeat that the young are religious,

and any form of religion justifies itself in
proportion as it appeals to the juvenile religious sense. And with or without any recognized form of religion, the young mind
will cling to fundamental religious principles. It is through the youth of France
that the recent much-spoken-of Neo-
Christian Movement is giving its greatest
promise. M. Vogue, as already quoted,
says that " that which strongly holds
these young minds is the instinct of the
correspondence between material things
and the profound invisible principles
which underlie them; it is the feeling of
community between men, the need of society according to that universal human
vibration which is the latent electricity of
the moral world." This exhibits the very
spirit of the Christian religion, and it
comes as an unintentional and powerful
argument for its adaptability to the human race. These young minds which
had inherited a prejudice to Christianity
from the infidel philosophy of the preceding generation, have, by a circuitous
journey, impelled by their own innate im-

pulses, and guided by their own reason, unconsciously returned to the underlying principles of the Christian faith. This is the kind of a movement needed in France. The editor of one of our American magazines sends up a lamentation over the comparative barrenness of our own land in such spiritual growths: "The feeling of the serious American," says he, "as he drops the record of this wonderful spiritualization of thought in France, this new birth of a nation, and he turns his thought home, is a feeling of sadness. There is no movement akin to this in our intellectual life." There is no such movement because no such movement is demanded in American life. But have we not a movement?—such a one as we need?—a movement against materialism to a higher spiritual and religious life? And is it not also among our young?

Yet, notwithstanding its natural sensitiveness to religious impressions and its spiritual fervency, youth is inclined to skepticism. But this very skepticism results from its restless, anxious search for the Absolute Truth. It is a reaching upward of the young soul toward the unknown God. It is suspicious of the means offered it by which to find Him. It impatiently pushes them aside. But it soon wearies in seeking for the "unsearchable," and either sinks back in gloomy despair, or finds God in the traditional faith. May our elders be considerate with the skepticism of youth. It is a healthy enough sign.

> "There lives more faith in honest doubt,
> Believe me, than in half the creeds."

Indifferentism is never skeptical. It willingly acquiesces in all the articles of the creeds to save being troubled. The skeptical mind is the mind that is troubled. It seeks the solution of its problems. Let it become active and alive and it will find all the solution it needs. "If any man will do his will," said Jesus, "he shall know of the doctrine, whether it be of God, or whether I speak of myself." The soil was fertile and ready for the seed which was sown.

In the next chapter we shall speak of the season of planting.

II.

THE SEASON.

"To everything there is a *season*, and a time to every purpose under the heaven."—*Ecclesiastes.*

"When they see the hours ripe on earth."—*Shakespeare.*

II.

THE SEASON.

IT is still more important that the seed be planted in the right season than that the soil be of the best quality. The moistened atmosphere, the vivifying sun, and the warm showers must all contribute their fostering forces to the germinating seed. It will matter little how rich and well cultivated the soil may be, if the seed is not sown in the proper season. This century came in with manifestations of great spiritual quickening in this country. Social and religious activity ran high throughout the world. It was the keen mind of Schiller which perceived that

"An epoch important has with the century risen."

Every part of this country had its religious agitation of some kind; in New Eng-

(31)

land the Unitarian reaction brought an
old theological controversy to a head and
break; in Kentucky the Great Revival,
the shouts of whose camp-meeting ecsta-
sies were caught up and echoed through
the forests of many a pioneer State, profoundly influenced the religious life of the
whole country, "increasing," according
to Dr. B. B. Tyler, "the membership of
the Presbyterian Church twofold, the
Congregational Church twofold, the Bap-
tist Church threefold, and the Methodist
Episcopal Church as much as sevenfold;"
and in the regions of the Ohio and Mis-
sissippi valleys, religious thought was
agitated to such an extent that the plea
for a return to the non-sectarian Christianity of the New Testament, as advo-
cated by Alexander Campbell, was received in the brief space of a quarter of a
century by between two and three hundred thousand people. But in all these
convulsions the controversies were of a
doctrinal character, and sect feeling was
accordingly intense and exclusive. To be
sound in the faith was of far greater con-

sequence than to be fervent in spirit in the service of God. Fraternal charity and Christian forbearance were graciously and nobly accorded to him who was weak in the flesh. A moral error was easily forgiven, but there was no kind of forbearance for doctrinal error. Heresy was inexcusable. This condition of religious America kept growing more and more intense until the outbreak of the Civil War, and the reaction against it which was then imminent was only staved off by that great national conflict, which drew the best energies of a generation from other channels to the solution and settlement of one all-absorbing political and social problem. A true picture of the state of American church life in 1852 is thus given by a discriminating and philosophic mind:

"We live in a sectarian and consequently in a controversial age. Christianity, as it is called, has degenerated into a speculative science, and therefore into innumerable forms of opinionism. Theories instead of *facts*, speculations instead of *faith*, forms and ceremonies in-

3

stead of a *new life,* and a profession of godliness without its *vitality* and *power,* are now and have long been the characteristics of the Christian profession." *

In these doctrinal controversies which were the weight of pulpit discourses, the burden of the religious journals, and even the theme of prayer-meeting talks and Sunday-school teachings, it is not to be supposed that the young could take much interest. Only by periodic revivals of feverish excitement were the churches replenished at all. The great bulk of the young men remained outside the church, and the depth of depravity and sin to which the life of the youth sank is sadly shown by the large number of lectures to young men which were delivered, published and distributed in those years.†
And the social life of the churches was

* Alexander Campbell in an address before the *Bible Union.*

† Henry Ward Beecher's *Lectures to Young Men,* published in a little western town in 1845, while he was but an obscure preacher, ran through an edition of three thousand copies in less than one year.

not attractive enough to hold the young, even when in protracted "seasons of religion" large numbers of them, in response to their naturally religious impulses had entered the Christian life. The frequent use of the unhappy appellation of "backslider" in their ecclesiastical phraseology is suggestive of the gloomy and pathetic state of religious life in those days. The Sunday-school was in quite vigorous operation, but there was no link which joined it to the church. There came a time in the life of every youth when he considered himself too big for the Sunday-school, and not yet old enough to acquiesce in the sober regime of the full-fledged Christian. There was a wide desert through which the waters of Christianity and church life had to run, and there was considerable leakage away into the sands of sin and indifference. It was a time in which the words of Byron might have found response in the breast of the thoughtful young:

> "Alas! our young affections run to waste,
> Or water but the desert."

The Young Men's Christian Association
was then in existence, but it was not vigorous or efficient; and even if it had been,
so far as its peculiar mission is concerned,
it would not have bridged the gulf. It
was a great and worthy organization which
grew out of the social needs of Christian
young men who are away from the influences of their home church and associa-
tions, or who are in need of Christian
companionship and life'in a good, moral
atmosphere. There was a deeper need
than this—it was the need of an influence
that would make the Christian life begin
at the mother's knee and continue until it
reached the grave. As Dr. Clark says:
"There is no reason why any child of
Christian parents should wander off into
the ways of sin and become befouled and
smirched in the ways of the world before
he can seek the purity of the kingdom of
God." Many people had said, and more
had thought something of that same kind
before, and yet children of Christian parents kept slipping away until in many fam-
ilies but the father and mother were pro-

fessed church members, even after their children were grown to manhood and womanhood. That something was wanted was very plain. And this want found expression in numerous societies of young people which were organized in wide-awake churches, and needed in thousands more. But, for the most part, the results of these efforts seemed to be only transient—they had not such a combination of elements as to make them permanent and strong. In short, the want was felt, but imperfectly expressed, until it found a lucid interpretation in one of the greatest organized movements of this century.

> " Deep wishes in the heart that be,
> Are blossoms of necessity."

As we have seen, the Civil War opened a valve of action for that surplus youthful energy which was otherwise either wasting itself or accumulating for a destructive explosion. And the two million young men who offered themselves on the altar of Mars in devotion to their respective factions, present a melancholy con-

trast to the two million young people,
who, in the various Juvenile Christian
organizations, are offering themselves in
a nobler and living sacrifice on the altar
of the God of true honor and righteousness. In the heat of that great conflict
no such movement as this could have succeeded. It was not the planting season
for the Christian Endeavor seed. Religious and intellectual movements are re-
served for the leisure and quiet of peace.

It was many years after the war before
the public mind could resume, with any
kind of real and earnest vigor, the suspended non-political matters. A new
generation has come upon the stage of
American life. The old abstract discussions of religious questions have returned.
Theology, such as it is, has come back for
its accustomed attention. This age is pro-
lific in theologians, destructive and constructive. We have the theological novel
now where we had the tale of politics and
humanity a half century ago. "Robert
Elsmere" has taken the place on our
shelves of "Uncle Tom's Cabin." Emi-

nent divines are talking of the evolution of Christian theology in pulpits which a quarter of a century ago thundered against human slavery, while the religious differences are not now denominational, but theological—no longer a quarrel between the sects, but a war between the conservative and radical schools of all the sects. The fight is becoming a hot one, and for many it is of absorbing interest, and yet the great bulk of our youth cannot be expected to take any real and vital interest in the conflict. But they must not be neglected while these discussions are going on. Indeed, it is in such seasons as these that they should receive most attention, for if any break is to come (and these are portentous times, if we are to believe our prophets) our only hope is in the staying powers of our youth. There are times when the ropes of faith become loosened by the very dryness of the atmosphere; when theology is troubled and its trumpet gives an uncertain sound. In such seasons as these, there is great danger that in the shaking up of our doctrines our spiritual life be lost, and in the general landslide of faith the foundations of our moral and social life be undermined; for, as Leslie Stephen says, "there is a correlation between the creeds of society and its political and social organization;" and if a creed is to be revised, or even die, we want to be prepared to cling still to our sacred and eternal principles of moral and social order. If in such seasons of disturbance and convulsion there is no great idea, no noble sentiment, that can come forward and inspire a high and disinterested enthusiasm, society, unable to reconstruct itself with the pace of disintegration, sinks back into moral exhaustion or indifference. So it was with France at the transition from the Old Regime to the New, and the youthful force, energy and power that has in France been lost to the world in a century which should have utilized it in a thousand ways and multiplied it a thousand fold only the eternal years will reveal. France is physically dying. Her population decreases with the passing away of each decade. Her rural districts, according to M. Taine, are fast relapsing into paganism. Her vitality has been poured out upon the sands. Her show of health is but the hectic flush of fever. She stood

> " Between two worlds, one dead,
> The other powerless to be born."

Says Canon Westcott in his *Social Aspects of Christianity*, " There are periods in the history of the Church—the history of the spiritual growth of humanity—which are at once an end and a beginning. . . . Unexpected forces reveal themselves and unexpected evils make themselves felt. Such periods are periods of intense, disordered, passionate feeling, *men's hearts failing them for fear and for expectation of the things which are coming on the world.*" This decade is such a period, and the Juvenile Revival has come as a God-send—like the white canvas of a sail to a vessel in distress, like the rope that is grasped by the drowning man. It is to the breaking up of this century what

the great work of Francis of Assisi was
to the period of the Renaissance, a comparison which we shall give fuller consid-
eration to in another chapter.

Another reason that makes this the
growing season for the Christian Endeavor
organization and life is that this age is
(strangely enough) both mechanical and
spiritual. The first half of this century
was a time of organizations of all kinds
and for all purposes. People ran wild
with the *penchant* for organization.
Channing humorously refers to this in a
discourse delivered in 1829: "It may be
said, without much exaggeration, that
everything is done now by societies. . . .
You can scarcely name an object for which
some institution has not been formed.
Would men spread one set of opinions
and crush another? They make a society.
Would they improve the Penal Code or
relieve poor debtors? They make societies. Would they encourage agriculture,
or manufactures, or science? They make
societies. Would one class encourage
horse-racing, and another discourage trav-

eling on Sunday? They make societies."
Though there is nothing so cold, lifeless
and uninspiring as the mechanical details
and burdens of organization, the multi-
plication of these societies has been the
outward sign of the inner life, spirit and
earnestness of the age. They were the
imperfect and cold expressions without,
of a warm heart within. Our complex
and extensive life made organization and
division of labor the two great social and
ecclesiastical, as well as economic, necessities. Even benevolence, which of all
things should come spontaneously from
the heart, finds its most satisfactory service in forms of organized and associated
charities. Organization has always been
the cold and rugged outer wall. To ex-
tremely spiritual and spontaneous natures
it has been a melancholy necessity. There
is no magnetism in organized order. It is
rather repellant than attractive. The systematic man is not the man we feel drawn
to, but, as Emerson says, "We love characters in proportion as they are impulsive
and spontaneous." In these last two de-

cades, thought and taste are becoming more spiritual. A half century ago a crabbed, unlovely dyspeptic, provided he had a powerful intellect, might have half the English-speaking world thronging at his heels, but to-day the men we follow are the men whom we can love. To-day the preachers whose pulpits we throng are men of fervent natures — warm-hearted human beings,—not disembodied intellects. The pulpit favorites of this generation have been such men as Beecher and Brooks. The favorites of a few generations ago were such men as Edwards and Chalmers. The good old times are returning when the dry eye of stoicism is no longer the necessary sign of manhood. Spirituality is more popular in this generation than intellectuality.

It was the union, then, of organization and spirituality, so that the latter vivifies the former, and the former's sole purpose is to serve the interests of the latter, that has met the wants of this age with peculiar adaptability and force. In the Christian Endeavor movement, organization has lost its repulsive ugliness by the light of a higher spiritual life which beamed through it. That the season was right and ready for the very seed that was planted, is seen in the fact that nearly every detail of the Christian Endeavor organization, as now supported by a million and a half people, remains substantially the same as in the original society.

The starting of this society was one of the happy accidents that so frequently occur in human history. The man who planted the seed could not possibly have foreseen what it would grow to. And it is that very circumstance that makes the movement, and the men to whom we are indebted for it, great. It is not a scheme that has been " pushed," but it is a seed which being dropped into the right soil at the right season has grown in spite of everything, until it has become a great tree with wide-spreading, sheltering branches. All truly great things are accidents. " There is less intention in history," says Emerson, " than we ascribe to it." No man or company of men can direct the current of history. Great men have been great because "their success lay in their parallelism to the course of thought, which found in them an unobstructed channel." Great ideas inspire great movements because they satisfy felt but indefinable longings, arouse latent energy, or speak the word which draws from a thousand throats the shout, "That's the idea! That's the idea!" But in dwelling on the Christian Endeavor idea we are infringing on territory which belongs to the theme of our next chapter—the *seed*. We are merely trying to show that there had to come a time when we were ready for the seed, as in the history of events there is a season prepared for the coming of every great idea. Three centuries before the coming of our Lord, the world was preparing for him. All that time the Roman cohorts were busy hushing the warring nations throughout the earth for the advent of the Prince of Peace, and Greek learning and language, like a soft carpet, were spread over the face of the earth. The ring of the closing doors of the Temple of Janus was heard throughout the world and quiet reigned. The eyes of all were turned toward the East when the Sun of Righteousness arose above those sacred plains. Man was waiting for his Saviour, and the happy shout, " Unto us this day a King is born—a Captain of our Salvation,"—which first reverberated among Judean hills has been the cry of every age for nineteen hundred years. It struck the popular chord; it interpreted the longing of the human heart; it gave man life. All other movements, however great, can be no more than miniatures of that greatest of all. And they are only great when they reflect the influence of that one, as the moon reflects the solar light. The flood of divine light then shed upon the world is sufficient for our richest, highest and completest illumination until the dawn of the Everlasting Day. To appropriate that light more and more as the years and centuries pass, until it has transformed the tissue of our being, should be the end of every human movement, for Christ truly came that we might have life and that we might have it more abundantly.

III.

.

THE SEED.

.

" The Kingdom of Heaven is like to a grain of mustard seed which a man took and sowed in his field."—*Jesus.*

" The stirring of the soil gives a chance for the growth of new seeds of thought."—*Leslie Stephen.*

4   (49)

III.

THE SEED.

Having taken a brief glance of the two preliminary objective conditions of the growth of Christian Endeavor, we are prepared to study the subjective elements whose combination in the Christian Endeavor scheme has given it the immediate sympathy, concurrence and confidence of the Christian youth of all denominations. The importance of the soil and the season is only relative. It is determined by the quality of the seed. The soil will not sustain us, and Autumn will bring us no fruits if the seed has not been sown in the spring time. Soil and season are but external conditions, lifeless circumstances, depending for their blessings to humanity upon the germs of life which they nourish. The seed is the liv-

(51).

ing germ which, by its operations on the
soil and the season, supports our lives.
It is the influence which binds us to outward nature. It is the regenerating principle which works, unseen, the marvelous
evolutions and changes in the vegetable
kingdom, as the eternal Logos, which is the
seed of God's kingdom, is producing
changes and evolutions in human life.

The movement of thought is slowly forward. She constructs institutions as they
are needed, and mercilessly tears them
down when their purpose has been served.
She reconstructs them when the change
of her position demands it, or leaves
them standing as landmarks to show the
course of her journey. When she has
need of any work along her highway of
progress she calls for it, and servants
from the roadside hedges appear to do
her bidding. Prophets, generals, kings,
reformers, all men of all talents, tendencies and professions, have answered to
her call. Impediments have been thrown
across her pathway, but she has ordered
them removed—and they have gone.

Fences have been built to change the direction of her motion and lead her off into narrow byways, but the fences have been levelled at her feet, and she has marched triumphantly onward. Alluring voices have called her to stop and turn backward, and she has seemed at times to halt and listen, but it has only been to resume her journey with greater vigor. Heavy weights have been thrown across her shoulders, but they have only increased her momentum. She is the invisible congregation, pressing onward to her union with her Lord. She is the Divine Life at work in humanity—God in the human soul. Her progress has been often clouded but never suspended. Her road led through a darkened wilderness. The mires and sloughs were about her and before her. The heavy rain stained and drenched her garments. The fiery eyes of savage beasts glared threateningly upon her. Only now and then a prophetic flash of lightning from heaven illuminated the way a few feet before her —then again all was dense blackness.

Her bitter wail pierced every corner of
the forest. She called for a Deliverer.
She called for Him in the Hebrew tongue
as her Messiah. She called for Him
in the Greek tongue as her Logos, or En-
lightener. She called for Him in the
Roman tongue as her Lord and Leader.
He heard her cry and came to show her
the true way. He left her His lamp to
be a guide unto her path and a light unto
her feet. She called for Luther, and he
obeyed her. Calvin, Knox, Wesley, all
have done her service. When she has
called for reformations, the church has
been broken and reconstructed. When
she has called for revolutions, nations
have trembled, political earthquakes have
followed, and governments have been
swallowed up, or brought to light. She
has cultivated the soil where the seeds of
human growths should be cast, and when
the planting season has come, she has
called for the seed and it has been
sown. This general trend of thought and
life is the omnipotent and irresistible
Zeit-Geist—the   Time-Spirit—and   all

minor movements have philosophic significance only as they are studied in their relation to this general forward movement, which, aided or hindered by external influences, has brought human life from the uncultivated garden of its creation to the civilization that adorns the threshold of the twentieth century. No social, political, or religious movement or agitation of any kind has ever occurred that has not been in some degree the resultant of some of the aggregated influences of this common trend; and on the other hand, the influence of every movement and agitation will be felt when the grand total is made up in the end of time. They are all contributing their forces to the general flow of human society. Sooner or later all the streams of influence unite themselves to the one universal current, and the current is affected by it. In the centuries of the crusades Oriental and Occidental life interchanged influences, and both East and West have felt the effects of the meeting, and always will. In the early part of this century the discovery of the sacred literature of the Eastern religions, through the medium of an ancient but new-found language, gave a new impetus to European thought; and influences which sprang from Indian philosophers three thousand years ago, and which no one two hundred years since would have thought could ever get beyond the Euphrates on the West or the Islands of Japan on the East, are now deeply stirring many centers of thought in Western civilization; while the forces of our ideas and the influences of our achievements—elements which had their birth in classic Athens, civil Rome, or the wilds of a German forest two thousand years ago, are irresistibly working their way into all currents of Oriental life, vivifying and transforming petrified nations by the introduction of a more potent and active leaven. Our libraries are being flooded with the sacred books of the East, and societies of Theosophy and esoteric Buddhism are springing up in the chief cities of Europe and America; while Christian ideas are taking

hold, with a much firmer grasp, of the
Eastern mind. Ideas, like men, must
bide their time. A naked idea may be
born in one man's mind and he may
preach it eloquently, fervently and confidently, but if no one else can understand
it, or sympathize with him, he is regarded
only as a crazy man or fanatic; he is
thrown into a dungeon or burned at the
stake, crowned with thorns and crucified,
or driven from his country, and his idea
seems to perish with him. But as time
goes on, the same idea may be born in
the mind of another man, and he preaches
it, no more eloquently nor confidently
than the first, but it gains adherents. It
falls like a spark in the dry tinder.
Thousands become his followers. What
is the reason for it? The reason is not in
the man, nor the idea itself; but in the
agreement and coincidence of the forces
and influences which make up and control universal life. • Forces which have
been latent, or only operating in a few
minds, suddenly by some wave of popular
influence are washed out in view of the

public gaze and become popular jewels. Christian Endeavor is simply one of the popular jewels of this generation.

Men sometimes sneer at what they call "waves of popular excitement," and great movements which have profoundly influenced society in their century and generation they sneeringly call "mere effervescences of passing enthusiasm." Such sneering is both unscholarly and egotistical. It is unscholarly and unphilosophical because it fails to catch the note of power that every movement must have before it can strike the popular chord, and if it seems to have struck the popular chord, we show an extreme of egotism when we deny that there is music in the strain for other ears, merely because our own have not caught it, or condemn the soul that has drawn inspiration from what might strike us as discord. Such sneering is also blind, so far as past human life is concerned, and if it has studied history at all, it has not studied it scientifically. All human progress has been by what may be called waves of popular excitement, or evanescent glows of enthusiasm; and it is the highest compliment that can be paid a great idea, to say that it has been able to be the inspiration of these same waves of popular enthusiasm, and to so direct them that they may serve their generation until their force has spent itself. And no man or movement ever served a passing generation and did not in that service bless all coming ages. All gloomy and unhappy pessimism would pass away if we threw ourselves into sympathy with the potent ideas of our times. Christianity was itself a growth of popular enthusiasm when it began, and no Greek or Roman philosopher or historian would have called it anything else. But it was an enthusiasm for a divine ideal—it was an abiding enthusiasm. It had its germ from God, and its roots were planted deep in the soil of the human soul. But every idea is a blessing, when its time comes, by its own innate worth. What, then, are the subjective elements in the Christian Endeavor seed which enable us to account for its power?

Christian Endeavor is a Protestant movement. Protestantism has all to gain from it. It supplies needs which had been felt only in Protestant churches. It feeds and satisfies the devotional hunger of the young which the mystic and symbolic worship of the Roman Church quiets and stupefies. The emphasis which Protestantism placed upon *faith alone* naturally resulted in defining the true nature and objects of faith in any number of different ways. In Protestant religion, therefore, theology became the predominating feature. It has been speculative and fluctuating, for faith, the object of its constant attention, has been ever-changing. It has made little of the æsthetic phase of religious worship, and the doctrine of works has been but secondarily considered. The Oxford movement was a reaction against it on æsthetic grounds. It went to work restoring the cathedrals and reintroducing the elaborate ritualism of the Mediæval Church. It was a morbid but a natural reaction. It was inevitable, but it has contributed no positive nor permanent blessing to humanity. The Christian Endeavor idea is both devotional and practical. While not in any way underestimating *faith*, the theme of its vigorous life has been *works*. It looks out upon a mundane existence and gives to it a religious aspect. It is systematic and business-like. It is natural that in its reaction from dogmatic Christianity it should make much of practical Christianity. It does not trouble itself about the theological question, "What must I believe?" but it starts with the question of Paul, "Lord, what wilt thou have me to do?" and in apostolic fervor it sets about reproducing Paul's life of active service. The great reactions of the present century have been doctrinal (or anti-doctrinal) in character; they have been negative or *protesting* movements, carrying out the spirit of Protestantism until it has almost become distasteful. Christian Endeavor is a reaction against the spirit of these reactions, and also the spirit which resisted them. These reactions were analytic in their general operation. They discovered new mines of truth and did good service in their day, but so deep had they gone in the analyses of their special differences that sectarian barriers had been heaped to great heights. Christian Endeavor is synthetic and catholic. It sounds the signal for the coming up out of the pits to mingle again in one common company. Twenty-five years ago when two Christians met, the first question which they mutually interchanged was, "Of what denomination are you?" But to-day when Christian Endeavorers meet—whether they are Baptists, Presbyterians, or Congregationalists—they forget for the time that they are anything more than Christians. And that man now who insists upon ringing the changes on doctrinal points, and pounding away on sectarian distinctions, soon finds himself without an audience. This whole movement is a keen and clear broadside against sectarian narrowness. This note of universality has been quickly caught up by the pulpit, which is always in the van of every good work, and in the great Christian Endeavor Conventions, Methodist, Episcopalian, Lutheran, and Disciple, are found sitting harmoniously in the same seats, while their respective pastors on the platform are vying with each other to see who can say the nicest things of the new drift. The first element, then, in the seed itself which has given it its marvelously rapid and extensive growth, is its synthetic and catholic spirit, as opposed to the analytic and narrow spirit.

The Christian Endeavor idea takes hold of the sense of *conscientiousness,* which is one of the most sensitive moral elements in juvenile life. Its aim is not to cultivate this conscientiousness, but it assumes it to exist and utilizes it. The conscience, or the sense of duty within us, comprises the chief part of the capital upon which the business of the Christian life is begun, and he who makes his sense of duty a thing too sacred to be harnessed and used, robs his practical life of its most valuable support. When the conscience revolted in the Protestant Reformation, it pulled away from everything characterized as Roman Catholic with such vigor that

when the fetters broke, its inertia landed
it on the extreme opposite ground. The
freedom of the conscience was then recov-
ered for all time. No power on earth will
ever again enchain it. It is God who has
wrought its liberation. It now believes
what it chooses, rejects what it chooses,
promises what it chooses. It has a right
to be free, but the question which Christian Endeavor asks is, "Has it a right to
be idle?" I knew a shiftless man in the
country. He lived in a little rented log
house, for which he was supposed to pay
$2.00 per month. He had a wife and
family. He was able-bodied and strong.
He cherished as an inalienable boon the
freedom of an American citizen. He
worked when it pleased him, which was
not often, and loafed the rest of the time.
When he worked at all he did only what
pleased him, for he was a free man. He
would never consent to labor under the
orders of another, for he was a free man.
Month after month of the summer passed,
and the harvests were calling for laborers,
but he was not in the working business.

He tinkered around his own house, because there he could be a free man. The shades and winds of autumn came, and the gorgeous-tinted leaves began to fall. The sound of rustling sheaves of corn, the clink of the hoes in the potatoe-field, and the melancholy quack of passing flocks of geese on their way to southern climates—all warned him of the approach of winter. But he still continued hugging his shadowy phantom—liberty. The cold blasts of winter came. The snow lay two feet deep. His children, half clothed, huddled about the broken stove. The wood-box was almost empty. The wind howled dismally without, and whistled through the cracks of the walls and doors, carrying streaks of snow across the floor. His wife, in a storm of rage, announces the unwelcome news that the cupboard is empty. She calls him a good-for-nothing wretch—worthless and negligent—and he cannot gainsay her word. He puts on his cap, draws it down over his ears, looks out of the window at the driving storm, shivers at the view, and goes out. He

5

calls on his nearest neighbor, and after sitting by the fire for two hours, talking about politics from the Revolution down, and how the boys in blue whipped the rebs at Gettysburg and Appommatox and Shiloh, he makes known his errand—he would like to borrow a few pounds of pork, and a little flour, and perhaps a little blackstrap molasses. But his frugal neighbor knows him, and he has neither pork, flour nor molasses to lend. So our friend goes on to the next neighbor, thus making the rounds of the neighborhood and returning in the evening with the scanty proceeds of his borrowing expedition to a starving family. He is free, but he starves on his freedom, because his freedom is idleness. So I have known it to be with some young Christians. "Come," it is said to them, "will you promise this?" "No, I won't make any promise. I will do it if it comes convenient, but I shan't make any promise; I am not going to bind myself. I shan't sign any pledge. I won't commit myself to anything. I'll do what I can, and I don't need to sign a pledge or contract, or make a promise. I want to hold my conscience free." This is the type of character which Christian Endeavor has had to deal with. As a movement, then, it means the inculcation of new principles of religious action. The Protestant doctrine of the freedom of the conscience has developed in many cases into the doctrine of personal irresponsibility, or the *idleness* of the conscience. This taking hold of the conscience—the sense of duty—and utilizing it in a religious vow or pledge, is bringing back into the service of religion an element in human nature which primarily belongs to it. "Religion," says Kant, "(as subjective) consists in our recognizing all our duties as Divine Commandments." That the Roman Church *abused* monastic vows in the Middle Ages is said by Christian Endeavor to be a puerile reason for our objecting forever to vows altogether. At any rate, the chief good which the Roman Church was enabled in former ages to accomplish came largely through her system of vows. That some

of her vows are abominable does not condemn the principle, and it is full time
that Protestants should begin to recover
from that individuating tendency which,
carried to an extreme, will bear the fruits
of unbridled anarchy—anarchy that even
now begins to threaten the destruction of
those vows and pledges which are the
basis of our moral and social order. The
Christian Endeavor pledge is one of the
strong features of the movement, and
gives to it a peculiar significance. Other
religious   movements   have   presented
creeds, either written or unwritten—an
enumeration of things to be believed or
denied—in which case they have all crystallized into denominations and been
added to the number of sects. Christian
Endeavor, instead of a creed, presents a
pledge. Assuming that the possibilities
of *faith* have been well-nigh exhausted,
she takes up her abode with her opposite
neighbor, *faithfulness.* The reasonable
hope has been expressed that the pledge
of Christian Endeavor will do for the
glory of religion among the youth of the

twentieth century what the knightly vow did for the glory of Chivalry among the youth in former centuries.

The Christian Endeavor idea is positive in spirit. It takes up its ground in affirmation, not in negation. What it can not affirm it takes no trouble to deny. Its tone is rather that of the New Testament than that of the Old. The Ten Commandments are largely prohibitions — "Thou shall not." The Sermon on the Mount is a beatitude upon those who are merciful, meek, pure in heart, peacemakers; upon those who, instead of concealing their light under a bushel, bring it out that it may shine before men—it is positive. This is the great distinction between the religion of Jesus and those of Buddha, Confucius and others. Buddha said: "The extinction of desire is the real self-conquest. To be fixed in spiritual contemplation is to conquer the power of evil." Jesus said: "He that *doeth* the will of the Father in heaven— he shall know the doctrine. He that *doeth* my commandments, he it is that loveth me." Buddha, in a striking parallelism to the Decalogue, says: * "Ten things are evil: murder, theft, lust, are evils of the body; evasion, slander, lying, flattery, of the speech; envy, anger, delusion, of the thought. Thou must not kill, nor steal, nor commit adultery, nor lie, nor be drunken. Avoid dancing, theatres, high seats, covetousness, costly dresses and perfumes." Jesus sums all this up in a positive form when he says: "This is my commandment, that ye love one another. These things have I spoken unto you that my joy might remain in you and that your joy might be full." Confucius said in his general law of life: "Never do unto others what you would not want done to yourself." This expresses negatively what the Golden Rule presents positively — "Do unto others what you would have them do unto you." One may sit inactive in his seat and obey Confucius; one cannot remain inactive and obey Jesus. The negative spirit be-

* The forty-two sections Sutra.

longs to the oriental mind; the positive
spirit to the Occidental mind. The theme
of Buddhism is *renunciation*, of Christianity, *life*. But the theology of the last
few centuries has rather tended to obscure
and belittle personal service as bearing
no weight in the scheme of religion. Man
has been rather thrown back upon negative ground as possessing no worth in
himself. Resolutions for the control of
conduct have abounded in restrictions—
pleasures to avoid and things to refrain
from doing. To such an extent was this
tendency carried that self-suppression, a
negative virtue of it, if a virtue at all, became the dominating law of life—an end
in itself. As it was wittily said, the extreme Puritanism opposed cock-fighting
and bull-baiting less because they caused
animals pain than that they afforded man
pleasure, and oftentimes sports that were
innocent and harmless were more emphat-
ically condemned than practices which resulted in both degradation and misery.
But this negative conduct of life was
never popular, and could not, by the very

constitution of the wide-awake, up-and-doing temperament of the European stock, long hold. It might, by the help of favoring circumstances, cling to a generation or two, but when the native element returns again which sees not the conditions that produced the negation of a century past, it must go. Christian Endeavor therefore also celebrates a resuscitation or rejuvenation of the positive element in religion. It substitutes obligations for restrictions; not a negative rule is given; every item of the pledge is positive. The bringing in of this positive element into the religious life of the young bars much of the skepticism natural to youth or deprives it of its seasoning, for skepticism is operative only in negation. With this brief study of the elementary principles in the Christian Endeavor idea—the germ of life in the seed, we shall more intelligently appreciate and sympathetically follow the phenomena of the movement—the growth of the blade.

IV.

THE BLADE.

(73)

IV.

THE BLADE.

THE Christian Endeavor movement can not at present be further than the first stage of its development. As it appears to us now, it manifests only the phenomena of a tender but promising blade. In an analysis of the idea we have also observed the favorable circumstances which surround it. Now the plant itself has been growing before our eyes for more than ten years. Now when we speak of the Christian Endeavor movement we include all minor and denominational organizations among the young which have re-expressed the Christian Endeavor thought, reproducing under other names its element of strength, save perhaps its catholic and synthetic spirit.

The fact that the idea has been widely plagiarized and its general organization and methods successfully imitated gives extra emphasis to its importance as a potent influence of the times. By the Juvenile Revival, then, I mean the general infusion of young life into the activity of the church in these recent years. And as Christian Endeavor is the exponent of this Juvenile Revival we make it the representative subject of our study. What the Christian Endeavor Movement is to this era, other movements have been to former eras, and we can fully appreciate its place in the religious thought and life of this decade only when we range it in line with the great movements of a similar character in other ages. The close of the nineteenth century presents some striking points of resemblance to the close of the thirteenth. Both are seasons of almost universal peace preceded by almost universal war. Both are seasons of widespread religious awakening and interest. Both celebrate a revival of Christian activities together with a *renaissance* in the one case of art and literature, and in the other of commercial enterprise and intellectual life. The former period is about three hundred years after the completion of Europe's Christianization. The latter is about three hundred years after the completion of Europe's re-Christianization in the Protestant Revival. A more detailed picture of the close of the thirteenth century will bring out this comparison more fully and enable us to appreciate better the strength or weakness of our own.

For two hundred years preceding the crusade period the church had no Christian activity to offer the scores of tribes and nations which she had Christianized. She had promised them conquest in the hours of battle, and when they returned triumphant from the field, confident that the Christian's God had given them the victory, they received the baptism of the church and offered her their swords to be consecrated to her service, for they knew no service but the service of the sword. Thus they turned their new-found zeal

against the heathen sheltered in the wilds
beyond the confines of Christendom, until all Europe was brought, more or less
by violence, into spiritual communion of
the church. But for two hundred years
after the completion of this great work
the sword had no fire of religious enthusiasm behind it—the sacred touch of the
church could no longer give it edge. For
two long centuries there was a general
restless sense of religious inactivity. The
poor Jews suffered then, and it was an
unfortunate time for the heretic. Religious indifference naturally followed this
universal idleness, and diversion and rec-
reation from the monotonous inactivity,
which the church seemed careless or unable to fill up, were found in bitter and
prolonged warfare between feudal lords
and rival royal houses. The long pent-up
force found a welcome outlet in the crusades, and the preaching of one religious
enthusiast was sufficient to raise all
Europe to arms, the flame even spread-
ing to the hearts of the children, who on
the banks of the Rhine assembled a vast

army of their number and marched south-
ward to the Mediterranean, perishing by
thousands and being carried off on the
way, until when they arrived at the sea,
only a fraction of their original number
remained to sail for the Holy Land.
Such a holy enthusiasm as that expended
in the crusades, had it been directed in
legitimate pursuits would have given a
different shade to the darkness of the
centuries which followed. It is a pathetic
picture. Poor, misguided man! filled with
a holy zeal, burning with desire to serve
his Savior with the highest service that he
knows, with the crimson cross upon his
breast, the stamp of religious fervor on
his brow, the shout of *"Deus vult!—*God
willeth it!" on his lips, dying on the
parched or malarial plains of an uncon-
genial clime, under an unfriendly sun, or
laying down his life before the cimeter of
the Saracen within sight of the white
sepulcher of his Lord, resigning all with
the faith of the martyr Stephen, whose
last words he utters with his dying
breath,—"Lord Jesus, receive my spir-

it "—in all this there is something pathetically sublime! Thus misery untold, sorrow and bloodshed unrecorded, were wrought by a Christian zeal which, otherwise directed, might have made us infinitely better, happier and more intelligent to-day. But as it was, the first, or the eleventh century crusade, ended in general failure and disaster; and as it does not require much of a set-back to cool a sudden and passing ardor, so the first crusade was followed by a period of extreme coldness and dissatisfaction with the church, which was itself affected by the general disappointed. Heresies multiplied; moral and religious torpor followed the disaster of the first crusade. Crime became general and society demoralized. Politics, which bore the natural fruit of a Machiavelli a few years later, was devoid of every sentiment which was not selfish and utilitarian. The condition of the church is thus vividly painted by Gieseler:

" While the system of ecclesiastical doctrines, with its progressive development, was enclosing the reason with bonds

ever narrowing, while at the same time
the means of salvation were more and
more losing their spiritual character and
their moral power by the one-sided speculations of schoolmen, and also sinking to
a lifeless mechanism in their administra-
tion; lastly, while this tortuous Church
system, despairing of any spiritual influence, was endeavoring to win recognition
for itself by continual acts of external
aggression; it could not but be that the
rebellions against the Church which in
earlier times came forward one by one
should now be growing more numerous
and more powerful." In the southern
part of France and the northern part of
Italy the Cathari, a devout and intelligent sect, spread widely and rapidly dur-
ing the twelfth century, and toward the
close of the century (1170) the Wal-
denses arose. Discarding speculative enthusiasm, they "aimed to realize again
apostolic Christianity and all its inward
devotion." The Scriptures were their
text-book, and so zealously and intelligently did they search them that they

6

were led far away from the ecclesiasticism
of their day. So popular were their plea
and their methods of preaching, and so
simple their mode of worship, that the
Waldensian heresy was received as a res-
urrection of the ancient Gospel. Thousands of the pious and intelligent among
the common people, the gentry, and even
the nobility heard it gladly. Rome became alarmed and thundered. But the
simple folk, strengthened by their scrip-
tural faith, replied that "they should
obey God rather than man." Such an
exasperating reply wrought their exter-
mination. They might have answered
the Jewish hierarchy thus, and been "set
at liberty," but they had no business to
speak in such style to the Pope of Rome.
In his simple and popular methods of
preaching, and going among the poor and
lowly, Peter Waldo gave the suggestion
and furnished the impetus to the greatest
benefactor of the Dark Ages—St. Francis of Assisi—who, in a movement composed of three orders, founded upon a
vow, not unlike the Christian Endeavor

pledge, illuminated a path of Christian service, the like of which had not before been seen since the close of the Apostolic era—a movement the influence of which we feel to-day. We cannot pass on without observing that a general appeal for a return to the simplicity of the apostolic faith and methods in religion has been usually followed by such general and lively interest in genuine and practical Christianity as the Franciscan and Christian Endeavor movements. Francis appropriated the elements of strength which he saw the Waldensian teaching possessed, without antagonizing the Church. He rather used them for her benefit in leading her on to a life of Christian activity such as she had not known before. In the nineteenth century the plea for a return to the simple Christianity of the New Testament has been more popular and potent than ever before in the history of Protestantism. The work of the Haldanes in Scotland, of the Disciples in America, whose marvelous growth has in less than seventy-five years carried their missionaries and Church to all parts of the globe; to say nothing of the various other movements, such as the Christian Connection in this country and the Bible Christians in England, having the same purpose before them,—all this is evidence enough of the truth of this assertion. Now the Christian Endeavor movement appropriates and combines the most practical and popular elements of these other movements, not to antagonize the existing forms of sectarianism, but to adapt them to the wants of sectarianism in such a way as to lead it to a more united and therefore a higher and richer life. What the Franciscan movement was to the thirteenth century, Christian Endeavor is to the nineteenth.

Let us draw this parallel still further. The close of the thirteenth century was the active period of the Renaissance. All the nations of Europe were awakening to a new life. Vernacular literature was rising over the ruins of the classics. The common people from the Mediterranean to the British Isles were growing into the consciousness of a common life. In Italy they had their Boccaccio; in England their Chaucer. They spoke in different languages, but both alike addressed their hearers in their vernacular tongues, and the tales that they told had the same foundations. Art, commerce and literature flourished on the shores of the Mediterranean; and in the North, colleges of eager students, numbered by thousands, listened to bold and learned professors. A grand and exciting age it was. The cords of life were drawn to high tension. But the danger to true religion and therefore to morality is always greatest in nervous times. "There was a terribly dark side to the age," says Canon Westcott. "The leprosy which was then the terror and scourge of the towns was the symbol of evils greater and more subtle which were eating into the heart of society. The Kingdom of God was on the point of becoming a kingdom of the world. The splendid churches which serve for the inspiration of modern art were too often built by extortion.

Religion was materialized both in its creed and its worship. Ecclesiastical jurisdiction was invading the whole sphere of life. The very consolations of faith were being degraded into a luxury for the wealthy. The poor—the poor, on whom Christ pronounced his first benediction,—were in danger of being forgotten.

"But the Spirit of Christ was not left without a witness. Preachers arose on many sides who vindicated for the Kingdom of God the claim to *righteousness and peace and joy.* For the most part their work was transitory because it was destructive, but one among them, Francis of Assisi, spoke in life so that his work can never cease to move."

To the Franciscan movement, more than to any other influence, is due the credit of having tided the Christian religion through the rapids of the Renaissance. As then understood, it hardly seemed worthy to survive the general reconstruction of things, but when the life and character of the humble Man of Naz-

areth were again brought into touch with
human life in all its relations by a sacrifice, devotion and spirituality which re-
vealed to man a new glory in himself,
Christianity again endeared itself to humanity with a still firmer attachment. It
is these surprising revelations of the
potency of our religion that dumbfound
and scatter her assailants. The speculations and apologetics of the schoolmen
could never have arrested the disintegration which had set in. But when a new
power showed itself in a great organization of earnest men and women who dis-
persed themselves among the poor, al-
leviated their suffering, shared their pov-
erty, preached to them the Gospel and
despised the very things which were then
the common craze—material wealth and
learning—the disintegration ceased and
the repair began, for it was an infusion of
fresh young blood into the arteries of a
dying church.

Our present period is a repetition of
much in the picture that we have drawn.
It is a critical age. We cannot expect

that the claim of sacredness is to shield a written page from the scrutiny of criticism. Criticism is in the air. That it is breathed in with every inspiration is the fault of no one. Examination of evidences is the spirit of the time. The higher critics are not to be *hushed* as children that are about to make some improper disclosure. They will speak out, and it is right they should, if they have any new truth to offer. If Moses really is not the author of the Pentateuch, we feel no horror in being correctly informed. Some claim that we have all the light now on that subject that we can have, and that opening the window will let in no more. Others claim that it will. Open the window, then, and if any light enters we are so much the gainers thereby; but if it is darker without than within, we have lost nothing. Apologetics and scholastic theology will do no more now than they did in the thirteenth century. Neither will orthodox scolding amount to much. The critic will only become the bolder; the heretic the more numerous; the scoffer

will scoff the louder, and through it all
the sinner will sin the harder. But they
are all beginning to stand still in wondering astonishment at the marvelous spec-
tacle of more than a million youth who
are alive with a fervent evangelical spirit.
Youth who were religiously either dead
or torpid spring up from the soil in a
mighty army as if by magic. From the
preacher in his study and the editor in his
sanctum, to the gambler at his table or
the drunkard in the saloon—all are talking about it. The Christian Endeavor
conventions eclipse in number, earnestness, and even enthusiasm, the political
conventions, and their mass-meetings are
seldom failures, rain or shine. Composed
of young people from a score of different
denominations, the most perfect harmony
prevails throughout the organization, and
discord seldom enters even into the com-
mittees. It has come as a new revelation
of the power of spiritual Christianity at a
time when her enemies were particularly
confident in their assertions that she was
really but little more now than a lifeless

carcass. They are hushed at its sight. That Christianity has yet a germ of life in it is proved by the vigorous blade that has grown up right before their eyes, and infidelity must own its prophecies falsified once more. David Hume on his death-bed disavowed any fear of death, but regretted that he could not live a few more years that he might behold the downfall of Christianity, that vast system of superstition against which he had employed the power of a gigantic intellect. It was a kind provision of Providence which did not permit him a view two hundred years intd the future, for his pretty delusion of the near collapse of the Christian religion would have been rudely torn from him, and he would have sunk back upon his pillow in· despair at the ˌprospect. No philosopher of his century so influenced English thought as he. And, cherished as his memory is by the thinking world, his conclusion concerning Christianity will not be received. And this one fact infinitely increases our respect for the power of the Christian faith. Many in these late years have reproduced Hume's prophecies of the approaching death of our religion. But this great Juvenile Revival has come as an opportune contradiction of their hopes—to guarantee the safety for a few generations more of the Ark of the Covenant.

The Franciscan order was also a lay institution. This was largely the secret of its power. Francis himself never received episcopal ordination. His rule was to the Franciscan movement what the pledge is to Christian Endeavor. The former is chiefly negative; the latter is positive. The former required the *renunciation* of all ill-gotten gains; *abstinence* from aggressive war and litigation; the *avoidance* of elegant dress and amusements. It also required meeting from time to time for worship and works of devotion. It was the negative principle in the Franciscan order that caused its decline almost immediately after the death of its founder. It did not take into sufficient account the element of individuality, as one of the essential facts of life.

Francis tried to destroy it. He once commanded that a rebellious brother should be buried, and when the earth had been thrown over him, he stooped down and asked, "Art thou dead, brother? Art thou dead?" "Yes," replied the poor fellow, "I am dead now." "Arise, then," said Francis, "I will have dead men for my followers—not living." All this is good enough in its place—the complete surrender of self—but it is only a preparatory step to something better and higher. When the pious young man came to Jesus, the first thing commanded him was the renunciation of riches, the goods on which his heart was set—self, in reality; but this was only preliminary to his taking up his cross and following his Master. All the Mediæval orders made too much of renunciation and not enough of life. It was the ascetic tendency which was the cause of their downfall. Looking over their ruins, then, it is gratifying to observe that none of that ascetic tendency, the germ of disintegration, is found in Christian Endeavor. It was not to take

life from us that Jesus came, but to give
us life, and that more abundantly. Christian Endeavor, then, so far as this char-
acteristic is concerned, has no fears of
decay. Other seeds of disease it may con-
tain which we cannot discern, but it will
not die of the same disease of which the
Franciscan movement died.

Another point of resemblance between
these two phenomena of religious history
is that both are eminently spiritual, and
both disavow any interest in intellectual
speculations. Francis would have nothing to do with learning. The Franciscan
interest in scholastics began only after his
death and with the decline of the movement. Dr. Clark has wisely and emphat-
ically expressed himself on this matter:
"It cannot be insisted on too strongly
that the Society of Christian Endeavor is
first and last and always a *religious
society*. It has social and other features,
but it is neither a social nor literary
society." It has been as a spiritual movement that it has succeeded. As an educa-
tional enterprise it would have done

but little. The mental education of our youth is very well looked after; it is the hunger of their souls that needs satisfying, and the success which yet awaits Christian Endeavor will be received only as it remains a spiritual force. "Spiritual life," says John Alzog, "even in the worst seasons, never entirely dies out in the church. When wants are felt new orders spring into life and supply them, and fresh energies are put into action." It is to supply a spiritual want that Christian Endeavor has sprung into life, and when it ceases to supply that want its mission will have ended, it will be consigned to the chambers of the past, and something else will arise to take its place.

There are many other movements in the history of the church with which Christian Endeavor might be profitably compared, but none that bear out the resemblance so minutely as the Franciscan. In 1119 nine young knights at Jerusalem constituted themselves into an ecclesiastical order, and took a vow of service to the church. This was the origin of the

orders of Knighthood which gave a religious aspect to war and chivalry, and
opened a field of activity for the fervor of
religious youth. Christian Endeavor possesses the chivalric devotion of the
Knightly orders, without their brutality
and licentiousness.

In 1384, Gerard Groot, of Deventer,
Holland, established an independent association which in its practical and devotional life presents many points of simi-
larity to Christian Endeavor. It was
composed of both clergy and laity, and
was called the *Clergy and Brethren of the
Common Life.* The members were young
men who "endeavored to promote Christian piety among themselves and others,
and worked for their end by fixed devotional exercises to which every one had
free access." It rapidly spread throughout the Netherlands and Northern Ger-
many. Its resemblance to the Young
Men's Christian Association is still more
striking. There has, for many reasons
which may appear obvious enough, been
no general movement of Protestantism

with which Christian Endeavor can be compared, for, with the exception of the Sunday-school and the Young Men's Christian Association, there have been no organized ideas that could break over denominational walls. Religious movements in Protestantism have nearly all been separative or sectarian. Christian Endeavor is aggregative, and therefore stands alone. It is not but a tender blade. The soil, the season, the sunlight have favored it. No insect seems to have touched it. What fruit it will bear in its maturity we shall leave to the fancy of another chapter.

V.

THE EAR.

"Then the *ear.*"—*Jesus.*

"Respect the promise of youth. The plant may stop at the blade without flowering; at the flower without fruiting."—*Confucius.*

V.

THE EAR.

HITHERTO we have been traveling on the solid ground of the past, the present, the known. We must in this chapter spread our wings upon the ether of the future, the unknown. We have nothing now to deal in but pure surmise and conjecture. But the field of surmise and conjecture is often more fascinating and fruitful than the field of fact. Our eyes are made for looking forward. The present does not seem to be enough for us to live in. The chief activity of life is in that which is prospective; while our repose is in retrospect. There is a calm, a quiet, a restfulness in past memories. They may bring us sadness, but they always bring us rest. It is like looking down the winding and rugged path of the mountain side up which we have climbed. But there is a nervous, exciting uncertainty about the future, that awakes us into the region of wondering expectancy, that gives us a feeling opposite from repose.

> " O, that a man might know
> The end of this day's business ere it come!"

is our constant and impatient prayer as with troubled brows we try to peer into the darkness of the future. It is like looking far up before us on the mountain-side over which we are to clamber, to discern the clouded summit. The past is dreamy; to indulge in its recollections affects us as a narcotic. The future is exciting; it affects us as a stimulant. Like the poor, little, unfortunate cuckoo, man is ever crying, " What will become of me? What will become of me?" But the future has more to offer us than gloomy forebodings. It is an inexhaustible storehouse of the treasures of the Infinite. What the future is to us depends upon the color of our minds. If they are bright, sunshiny and hopeful, the future is our chief source of joy, for Hope smiles over ruin and desolation, and even "lights her torch at Nature's funeral pile." But to the mind of a somber and melancholy hue, the future is like the dreaded darkness of the night, filled with prowling beasts and uncanny terrors.

But personal hopes and fears shall not concern us here. As wave upon wave of influence comes rolling upon us, driving us hither and thither, but with a general forward movement—finding ourselves no two moments in the same spot—the standing question of human life is as to "where we are and whither we are tending." That question never grows antiquated, for the point from which it is viewed is ever changing. We are either hopeful or wary or suspicious of every tendency. We speculate on the natural results of a thing, whether it is likely to do good or evil. We hopefully engage in enterprises for years without receiving any return for our service, because of the promise they give forth.   What will be the fruits of Christian Endeavor?

Religious life has already been greatly quickened and enlarged by the influence of Christian Endeavor, but what we have received is not even an earnest of the harvest yet to be. In this chapter we shall consider some of the real results that are sure to come in less than a generation from this one decade of Christian Endeavor. The first practical result will be political. In a republic-democratic country like America, politics is king. From the little boy in dresses who shouts for his candidate before he can speak his own name, to the octogenarian who cast his first vote for Andrew Jackson, politics is all. It is the rule among us that all the time and attention which we can expend outside of the pursuit of our livelihood are devoted to politics. Religion has suffered, literature has suffered, general culture has suffered from this all-absorbing subject that demands and receives the bulk of our leisure. Christian Endeavor has been able to draw the attention of youth from the fascination of political and national matters to religious themes, and it is high time that the stringent pressure of politics on the juvenile mind should be relieved and replaced by a healthier and less dangerous force. American politics is in danger of becoming a system of wire-pulling, unscrupulous chicanery and unshamed dishonesty. An honest old man in politics may occasionally be found, but the younger instalment of politicians are for the most part a set of cunning manipulators. It is the legitimate fruit of the influences of a generation back, when the President's chair in glittering colors was held before the easily corrupted imagination of every school-boy; when to be member of congress, governor of a State, mayor of a city, or sheriff of a county was the noblest kind of incentive offered to juvenile industry. This teaching is now making itself felt in the wild and conscienceless scramble for the richest prizes and the highest seats. From teachers, books and newspapers came the old and oft-repeated story of how Lincoln, Grant and Garfield, from humble log cabins, found their way to the White House. Our childish fancy was filled with the thoughts of the presidency as the end and aim of life. The dome of the Capitol haunted us in the daytime, and in our dreams we were driven in four-horse open carriages, bowing blandly, hat in hand, to the thronging masses on either side, through which the marshals of the day made room for our advance—with the mayor and the city officials in the rear. We declaimed, *a la* Daniel Webster, from bowery platforms, and held spell-bound by our matchless but imaginary eloquence the broad acres of mouth-open multitudes. It was my aim to sit in the President's chair, and then, Napoleonic *coup d' etat*, convert the republic into a mighty empire to be mine and my heirs' forever. My object was so solely the presidency that if my parents or anybody else wanted me to do anything, my first thought was, will it help me on in my race for the White House? How well do I remember of my father holding me on his knee and trying to remove from my mind that horrible delusion, and telling me of a certain Henry Clay, a great statesman, who said "he'd rather be right than be a president." And I remember I thought, what a fool that man must be! And the delusion never did completely leave me until I became old enough to look about me and see that there were ten million boys in the United States, all scrambling for the same office, and it was so clear to my mind that we couldn't all sit in the president's chair, with any sort of comfort, that I concluded to retire to private life. But even yet the old flame revives sometimes and, in a heated presidential campaign or nominating convention, I feel like coming forward and presenting myself as a dark horse, or permitting some friend to state that I will sacrifice my personal wishes at the altar of the party's interests and have consented to take the field.

I would not have been thus personal did I not think that my own experience has been that of the majority of American boys. Let us hold the words of two poets before the eyes of our youth as a motto safe and inspiring:

"An honest man's the noblest work of God."

To be a *man* is more than to be simply president, senator or general. The title of Jesus Christ which he most loved and which crowned him with the greatest glory was Son of *Man*. He was not the son of a king, nor the son of Rome, Greece nor Judea, but the simple and therefore sublime and perfect Man!

Politics is immensely attractive to the young, for the young are hero worshipers, and nothing like politics supplies the juvenile fancy with heroes. But to make heroes of even the best of men is dangerous. For in imitating them we are more likely to reproduce their faults than their virtues. Much greater is the danger in politics where so few men are worthy objects of that adoration and whole-souled allegiance which the fervent young heart will pay to some person. The man who can carry out a shrewd piece of political engineering to a successful issue will always be a fascinating personage to the young men who are idle spectators of the machinery of politics, but for all our boys to turn shrewd political tricksters would make this country a generation hence altogether too mean to live in. Boys will be what their ideals make them. We are rejoiced then to see that the young people of America are beginning to turn their eyes from the skirmishing grounds of politics, where treachery, robbery and general knavery become familiar sights to them, to the greater battle between sin and righteousness, where they may gather around the standard of One whom they may safely make their Ideal, of One who for nineteen centuries has been the inspiration and elevation of humanity, the glory of our race. If we become what our ideals make us, we may expect something nobler, grander and more manly in the political life of a generation ahead than we see in that of today. God introduced to the world in Jesus of Nazareth an ideal picture of humanity. It was the crowning glory of the divine life in man. The enthusiastic devotion and imitation which that picture inspires are worth more to us than all the learning of Greece, the civic glory of Rome and the commerce of England; for the religion of Christ has raised up from among the barbarians of the North, men more learned than the Greeks; the discipline and order of Rome have been far excelled; and the commerce of our nation now infinitely surpasses that of the whole ancient world. We do not need to state our belief that all this is due to the influence of the Christ-life in Europe, for it is sufficient even to know that these marvelous results have not been impossible under the influence of that Life. Politically, then, and nationally, we have much to hope from the return of the Christian religion to a claim upon the hearts of the young. Let Jesus, our ideal Man and our Savior, be the theme of the young, and the world is safe. If "Christ for the World" is the motto of our lives the world is not likely to suffer.

The first blessing, then, to which we call attention to result from Christian Endeavor will be political and national in character. But a blessing which is simply of a national nature should not satisfy the Christian. It seems narrow and small for us to consider such things from a political standpoint, and if Christian Endeavor has nothing more by which to commend itself to us, it is not worthy of all that has been said in its favor. But here is where it opens itself out to us in its broader view. It is cosmopolitan in spirit.

From a cosmopolitan and humanitarian point of view there is considerable reason to fear from the national sentiment, as it seems to be manifesting itself in these days. When any sentiment which is not wide enough to take in all men becomes a controlling sentiment there is always danger. The love of some men extends only to the bounds of their nation. They love their country and will die for her, but would rejoice in the humiliation of another. They will march through fire and slaughter under the flaunting Stars and Stripes, but the banner which another man loves they would tear to shreds. They grow white with indignation and call for arms when they read of the Baltimore massacre in Valparaiso, but when they are asked about the New Orleans massacre they express only a calm regret or find refuge in making explanations. They declaim with heart-thrilling feeling those patriotic words of Scott,

"Breathes there a man with soul so dead," etc.

But they would stumble if they attempted to quote our Lord's commission to his Apostles, sending them into *all the world to preach the gospel to every creature.* They can put more spirit into the singing of the "Star-Spangled Banner" than into "Praise God, from whom all Blessings Flow." Such men we call patriotic men. We glorify their names. We raise monuments in their honor. We inscribe poems to commemorate their deeds. We fill the pages of history with records of their lives and performances. Right and just though all these plaudits may be, is there not a grander sentiment than even that of patriotism—a sentiment that is not confined to national boundaries—a sentiment that takes in every child of God in its all-embracing love for humanity? It is the cosmopolitan or humanitarian sentiment caught from the heart of Jesus Christ, who cherished neither sectarian prejudices, national partialities nor special sympathies, but whose sympathy was universal, boundless as God, and free. Why should my brother on the other side of the national line be less entitled to my fraternal love than the brother on this? Is not patriotism a sectional feeling spread out over a broader territory? It is a noble sentiment, for any sentiment which is broader than selfishness is noble, but it is not so noble as that of philanthropy. John Howard was a better and greater man than Lord Nelson, and Jesus was greater than Alexander. Sectarian bigotry is love extended to the limits of a sect. Partisanship is love extended to the limits of a party. Patriotism is love extended to the boundaries of a nation. The broader it grows the grander it becomes. Christianity is love universal; it takes in God and man.

The threatening danger to Europe to-day is the intensifying of the national feeling. The national armies are growing stronger as patriotism grows hotter. International commerce and travel break down no national walls. The Prussian and the Frenchman, the Briton and the Russian scan each other's motions now with greater suspicion than ever before, while all Europe listens in breathless silence for the distant rumble of approaching war. Let this pent-up national feeling and energy continue to rise until the floodgates give way, and a torrent like that which swept down the Conemaugh Valley will deluge the nations of Europe. This fear of war is not mere "newspaper talk." It is the talk also of cool-headed philosophers. Ernest Lavisse, professor at the Sorbonne, in a work published a short time ago, says that "the

expectation of war is one of the principal
phenomena of our present civilization.
It manifests itself in the system of armed
peace.   Formerly peace wore only demi-
armor; to-day it is armed from head to
foot.   Without any effort, by a tap of
the telegraph, after some puffs of loco-
motives, there is a war; and what a terri-
ble war!   .   .   .   The feeling that a few
dawns may suffice to illumine the desper-
ate conflict and the death of a fatherland
weighs heavily upon Europe.   There are
countries in which the cruel cry *vae victis*
is ready to burst forth from men's
breasts."*   That something should be
done is plain, and whatever is done must
come through the welding influence of
Christianity.   The chief mission of our
religion on earth is to supplant selfish,
narrow and sectional sentiments with a
broad human sympathy.   Early Christianity extinguished the flame of sectional
and national feeling and substituted for

* Vue Generale de l' Histoire Politique de l'
Europe.
8

it a wide human fellowship and love. So potent was this cosmopolitan spirit in the early Church that even the inflexible exclusiveness of the Jew with its inborn prejudices was laid aside under the vision of that heavenly truth that "God is no respecter of persons." The barriers of nationality gave way before it and in Christ there was neither Jew nor Greek. The vast imperial power of Rome, which held the world in prison chains and strengthened her own nationality by exterminating other nationalities, enervating and destroying humanity from Carthage to Britain, began to crumble and decay under the oxygen of the Christian faith. Christianity must be universal in spirit or its essence is gone. The Church can become neither Greek, Roman nor Anglican without becoming at the same time unchristian. Its greatest service to humanity, as such, is lost when it becomes nationalized or specialized in any way. Its death knell as a Christian Church was rung when Constantine succeeded in appropriating it to the support of the Empire. Christian Endeavor has taken hold of the essence of Christianity again, and this has made it at once unsectarian and cosmopolitan. It is as much at home under the Union Jack as under the Stars and Stripes. Dr. Clark's missionary tour around the world is but an outward expression of the inner spirit which governs the movement. The feeling of this age is humanitarian and cosmopolitan. This is shown in the great love in which such preachers as Channing and Beecher are held. The right word now spoken which will embody this feeling in a tangible form will do a glorious philanthropic service. That word is found in the Christian motto of the Endeavor organization. "One is your Master, even Christ, and all ye are brethren."

Another one of the fruits which the next generation will enjoy from Christian Endeavor will be an invigorated church life. If the present indications count for much, the problem of the unchurched masses will then be practically solved. Church energy will not be so likely to be expended in denominational competition, but it will go where it can supply the greatest needs. Already the young people of the Christian Endeavor Societies of many churches are doing missionary work, preaching the gospel to those not situated so as to attend regular Sunday services. They are building churches even in many towns and cities where there is greatest want of Christian teaching.

We have here mentioned but a few of the practical or social fruits which we are likely to enjoy as the result of this movement—its blessing to general human society in bringing man nearer to his brother, and binding them into a stronger and more delightful union, and by weakening some of the evil elements in the social and political department of life. If the effects we have prophesied come, we shall have no reason to be surprised; but if they do not come, it will be a case of "the blade stopping at the flower without fruiting."

VI.

THE FULL CORN.

" Then the full corn in the ear."—*Jesus.*

" Unto the fullness of the measure of the stature of Christ."
—*Paul.*

(117)

VI.

THE FULL CORN.

IT would be too much for us now to pre-
dict what will be the fullest and ripest
fruits to fall from the Christian Endeavor
tree in the times that are yet to be. It
promises much, but with our limited
knowledge of the laws of cause and effect
we cannot know that its promises will be
fulfilled. Our greatest hopes in Christian
Endeavor will not be realized if it has
nothing for us beyond a purification of
national life and a widening of the humanitarian sentiments. As has been said
already, its purpose is primarily and dis-
tinctly religious. Its mission is to bring
out the possibilities of the human soul in
all its beauty and perfection of development. It is an expression of dissatisfac-

tion with the philosophy of the earthly, and a longing again for the things that are heavenly, eternal, and that fade not away. It is the return of the spirit for its share of attention. It is not satisfied with railroads, and telegraphs, and real estate, and dry goods, and groceries. It has no quarrel with these things, but it calls for something more. It calls for faith, for hope, for love, for truth, for righteousness. In short, it is a cry for God. As the infant who wanders away from its mother and is lost in the forest, though the harmonies and beauties of nature are singing in its ears and dancing in its eyes, it is not contented and will not be comforted. The very flowers whose gorgeous hues would have been its delight, had its little hand been clasped in that of its mother, are a mockery to it in her absence. There is no melody in the songs of the birds without its mother. You may offer it rattles and candies and pictures in vain. It wants its mother. It appreciates these things in its mother's presence but not in her absence. We children of the Infinite Father are very much like the little infant. We delight in factories and farms, in books and colleges, in canals and steamships while we are in sight of our God, but the moment we have wandered farther away than we intended and are brought suddenly to realize that we are alone in the world, we then leave wealth and family and fame and all, and cry out for God. Nothing then short of God will satisfy us. This is the cause of all the pathetic pictures of religious fanaticism painted on the pages of our race's history. The heathen mother who casts her child in the flames beneath the outstretched arms of her deity; the grim Druid priest whetting his knife under the broad branches of the sacred oak for human sacrifice; the gloomy crusades; the howling and dancing dervishes;—all these and many more nearer us are sad illustrations of the human heart, having lost sight of God, seeking by fanatical extravagances to find him again. An era of religious activity is the logical consequent

of an era of indifference to spiritual
things. The farther away a people have
wandered from God and into materialism
the more violent will be the cries and
struggles to find him when the reaction
sets in. A nation that would avoid the
perils of religious fanaticism should avoid
the extreme of spiritual indifference.
Whoever, therefore, would preserve a
calm, even and peaceful national religious temper, will rejoice that the threatening materialistic tendencies have been
opportunely arrested by a calm but fervent and intense religious feeling that has
taken possession of the generation which
will be responsible for the to-morrow of
the race. The spiritual losses we have
sustained in the deaths of nearly all our
great poet-philosophers and preachers
must be compensated for. The loss of
our Emersons and Carlyles, our Tenny-
sons and Brownings, our Longfellows,
Lowells and Whittiers, our Beechers,
Spurgeons and Brookses, has been a tre-
mendous spiritual drain on the race, and
we can ill afford to do without them at

this time. We are losing our Emersons and getting Edisons instead. How long we could keep up such a trade would be hard to tell. Even now the question is being asked by the practical mind, What good is philosophy? Of what practical value are literature and dead languages? How does a study of Homer, Milton or Shakespeare enable one to make any better living—except as he intends to teach those things? These are some of the questions now commonly asked which show how completely materialistic considerations are beginning to control our thinking and acting. The tendency which they reveal is a pernicious one.

The next questions to be asked will be, Of what practical value are culture and virtue? Indeed, too scrupulous conscientiousness is oftentimes unprofitable in business and politics. To lie possesses a commercial value. What *use* have we for religion? This view of things has crept into the church. How may I make church membership a means of advancement, of prosperity to me? How may I turn my prayers and my long face and my Amens and my Sabbath street-carried Bible into dollars and cents? Do we understand, therefore, that when religion comes to possess no commercial value it is to be abandoned? Then we will come to ask, What profit is there in love—love for father and mother, for brother and sister, for wife and children?' We can easily see that this tendency carried out to its logical issue would land man again among the brutes. This is a retrogression. Instead of falling backward toward the protozoa, we should press on to the continuance and completion of the evolutionary process, until we come in the unity of faith and the knowledge of God's Son unto that perfect manhood, unto the fullness of the measure of the stature of Christ. The Christian Endeavor movement is, therefore, a refreshing sign of our present spiritual vitality.

The one Convention held in New York City in 1892 is an event for future historians of American life to study. It was an epoch in the history of our nation. It

calmed the fears of the thinking minds
that were alarmed for the spiritual future
of the race. It quieted the loud claims of
the enemies of our faith that Christianity
was losing its hold on the people. Altogether it gave quite a new coloring to the
general condition of things. It was one
of these needed surprises that come now
and then as regenerating influences to a
nation. In accordance with this event
many have been compelled to readjust
and modify their philosophy of things.

The highest and best results of this
wonderful movement will be to fill up the
mould of humanity—to lead man closer to
his God, the fountain of all that is divine
in man—

" That God, which ever lives and loves,
  One God, one law, one element,
  And one far-off divine event
  To which the whole creation moves."